OLIVIA

AND
THE PROVERBS

By
Pat Guy

ISBN: 978-1-8382927-2-0

Illustrations: Alessandra Covino

Olivia's pictures: Jamie Buddle and Ruby Parrish

For Holly, Amy, Toby, Ruby, Jamie, Theo and Reuben.

CONTENTS

Understanding proverbs will help children to develop their reading and listening comprehension.

A proverb is a short sentence, which gives advice or tells you something about life. Because proverbs have different levels of meaning, they can be used to introduce children to inference or 'reading between the lines'.

For example: -

The proverb, 'No use crying over spilt milk', has a literal meaning. If you spill milk, there would be no point in getting upset, because it would be impossible to put the milk back into its container and nothing could be done to improve the situation.

The proverb's non-literal meaning is broader, namely, it is pointless to be annoyed about something that has already happened.

In the same way, the proverb, 'Look before you leap', contains non-literal advice about thinking before acting.

The proverb, 'The proof of the pudding is in the eating', implies that a pudding may look tasty, but when you eat it, you realise it is bland and flavourless. The underlying meaning of the expression being that the quality of something can only be judged after it has been tried.

Proverbs can teach children a useful lesson about the alternative meanings behind what people say or words that are written on a page.

Olivia and the Proverbs

Olivia is a little monkey who lives with her Mummy, Daddy, older brother Pip, older sister Violet, and the family dog Biscuit, in a house near the middle of town. Olivia's Daddy works in an office; her Mummy draws pictures for magazines; and Pip and Violet go to school.

Olivia is friend with everyone, but her best friends live in an old people's home, the Honeypot Home for the Retired. The Honeypot Home is in the big house next door to Olivia's house. Olivia often goes to see the old people who live in the Honeypot Home. She sits with them in the garden when it is warm, or in their big sitting room when it is chilly.

Olivia's family.

mummy

daddy

Biscuit

Violet

pip

Olivia has two very best friends at the home. One is an old monkey called Boris. Olivia and Boris enjoy going into town together; having cups of tea at cafés and sampling different cakes. Boris is interested in gardening, and Olivia likes to chat to him while he tends the plants in the Honeypot Home's garden.

Her other best friend is Blossom, an old lady monkey, whose room is on the top floor of the Home. Blossom says Boris has green fingers, which is Blossom's little joke because Boris's fingers are brown. Blossom's room is full of interesting trinkets and a birdcage for Joey, her budgerigar.

Olivia's friends.

Elsie

mabel

Blossom

Boris

CHAPTER 1

The Dog Show

(Beauty is in the eye of the beholder)

Biscuit, Olivia's dog, is rather plump and a little bit lazy. Although he does like to go into town with Boris and Olivia, Biscuit isn't keen on walking far. He is too heavy to carry, so when he gets tired, Boris and Olivia lift him into Boris's shopping basket on wheels.

At first Olivia thought Biscuit might not want to walk because he didn't like getting his paws muddy, so she made him some shoes from Pip's old football socks, but the shoes didn't make him better at walking. Then she thought it might be because he didn't like getting his tummy dirty, so she made him a suit from a black bin liner. Biscuit was a patient dog and lay very still while Olivia measured him, and then tugged his paws through the holes she had made in the bin liner.

Olivia didn't realise Biscuit had fallen asleep until he began to snore.

One sunny morning Olivia was sitting in the Honeypot Home's garden with Blossom. She had put a towel around Biscuit's shoulders while they played at hairdressers. Blossom had given Olivia an old hairbrush and hair curlers, and Gladys had given her some old hair clips. Olivia was brushing Biscuit's soft fur carefully into little bunches.

'Oh look,' said Blossom suddenly, pointing to some writing in the newspaper. 'A Dog Show. I wonder if Biscuit would like to enter one of the competitions.'

'I'm sure he would,' said Olivia. 'He's bound to win.'

The next Saturday afternoon, Blossom and Olivia took Biscuit to the Dog Show. There were lots of smart-looking dogs, and Olivia looked doubtfully at Biscuit in his bin liner suit. They walked past some tall, slim poodles who made Biscuit look a little short and tubby.

'Mmm, the most agile dog in the show. There's not much point in entering him for that,' said Blossom, struggling to push Biscuit across the grass in Boris's shopping basket on wheels.

Biscuit could see some dogs weaving in and out of poles and running up and down ramps. It made him feel dizzy, so he shut his eyes.

'Biggest bark?'

Biscuit looked nervous.

'That would be no good, he's frightened of loud noises,' said Olivia.

'Most obedient? Oh dear, I don't think we can enter him for that one either.'

'Maybe we'll just watch everyone else,' said Blossom. 'We can't make Biscuit into something he's not.'

Olivia and Blossom found a bench and sat down with Biscuit to watch everything that was going on.

Blossom heard the music from an ice cream van and went to buy two ice cream cornets. They sat together on the bench in the sunshine with their ice cream cornets watching the other dogs. Olivia pointed out a little fluffy puppy to Blossom and, while Blossom had her head turned, Biscuit leant across and swallowed her ice cream in one single gulp.

It was such a funny thing to do that Olivia and Blossom couldn't help laughing. Biscuit looked at them quizzically with ice cream all over his nose. One of the Dog Show judges with a big camera hanging round his neck, took a photograph. It was a lovely photo and the man was very pleased. Biscuit didn't win any of the difficult competitions, but he did win the 'Funniest Dog in the Show' award and a shiny, yellow rosette. Olivia pinned the rosette onto Biscuit's bin liner suit and when Blossom and Olivia got back home, they put the rosette above his bed.

'You see, Olivia,' said Blossom. 'Everyone is good at something.'

CHAPTER 2

Going Camping

(A friend in need is a friend indeed)

Olivia's big brother Pip was going camping for the weekend with his Scout group. Olivia was upset because she wanted to go camping too.

'We haven't got a tent that is big enough for all of us, Olivia,' said Daddy, 'and you are too little to go camping by yourself.'

'But we have got a tent,' said Olivia. 'We've got the wigwam that Grandma gave me for my birthday.'

'Yes, I suppose that is a sort of tent,' said Daddy, 'but it's really just for playing in the garden, not for going camping.'

'Maybe we'll borrow a tent and go camping in the summer,' said Mummy. 'Perhaps you could camp in the wigwam in the garden tomorrow.'

'No,' Olivia said rather crossly. 'You have to go camping in the Great

Outdoors. I've seen the pictures in Blossom's holiday brochures.'

'Maybe you could camp out in the Honeypot Home,' Daddy laughed.

'Mmm,' said Olivia with a thoughtful look on her face. 'I'll go and ask Blossom.'

'Now look what you've done,' said Mummy. 'Poor Blossom.'

Olivia came back ten minutes later.

'Blossom says, "Yes."'

Mummy went upstairs and found some pillows and blankets, while Daddy took the wigwam down from the top of Olivia's wardrobe.

Mummy carried everything round to the Honeypot Home and spoke to Blossom.

Olivia had her bath, found some clean pyjamas, her dressing gown and slippers, and got her haversack out of the wardrobe.

'Biscuit will have to come as well,' said Olivia. 'He told me he would like to go camping.'

Daddy and Olivia carried a puzzled-looking Biscuit round to the Home in his dog basket and up the stairs to Blossom's room.

Olivia emptied her haversack out carefully onto the carpet in Blossom's bedroom.

'I asked Pip what I would need,' she told Blossom.

'That was clever of you,' said Blossom. 'You do seem to have packed rather a lot.'

'Yes,' said Olivia importantly. 'Pip said you have to be prepared for all eventualities. That means you have to be ready for anything, Blossom. Blizzards, wild animals, forest fires.'

'I don't think I get many of those in my bedroom,' said Blossom.

'Mmmm,' said Olivia with her nose still inside the haversack. 'I think that's everything: a whistle, a torch, a bottle of water, a packet of biscuits, woolly hat and warm gloves.'

She put on the hat and gloves.

'The biscuits are a bit squashed,' said Olivia. 'I better eat them now.'

'No, no,' said Blossom quickly. 'They look rather crumbly. I'll bring you some better ones from the kitchen.'

Ten minutes later Olivia had put up her wigwam and laid out the pillows and blankets to make a little bed.

'Do you think you'll be comfortable?' asked Blossom.

'Oh yes,' said Olivia. 'My wigwam looks very cosy. I think I'm going to like camping.'

'I'll just go downstairs to watch the News,' said Blossom. 'I can't quite see the television from my chair with your wigwam in the middle of the carpet. I'll be back up to go to bed as soon as the programme finishes.'

'Oh, I expect me and Biscuit will fall asleep quite soon,' said Olivia. 'Camping makes you very tired.'

'That's good,' said Blossom, switching off the light.

'Don't turn out the light please, Blossom. Biscuit is frightened of the dark.'

'I'm sorry,' said Blossom. 'I'll leave the bedside light on for him.'

'Yes please, and could you leave the door open? We like to hear people talking so we don't feel lonely.'

'Alright dear,' said Blossom as she went out of the room.

'Oh, and Blossom,' said Olivia, 'please can you tell everyone not to make a lot of noise when they go to bed in case they wake us up.'

'Righty-ho, dear,' said Blossom, and went downstairs.

When Blossom came back upstairs ten minutes later, Biscuit and Olivia were fast asleep and snoring quietly. Olivia was in the wigwam and Biscuit was curled up on the end of Blossom's bed. Blossom tried to push him off the bed and into his basket, but he was too heavy.

Blossom sighed and went into her bathroom to have a wash and brush her teeth. She put on her nightie, edged her way carefully around the wigwam and got into her bed in the space above Biscuit.

She couldn't help smiling. This is so silly, she thought to herself. I don't suppose many people have a wigwam in the middle of their bedroom. Oh well, at least I have a lovely soft hot water bottle, and she put her feet on Biscuit's warm back.

Biscuit and Olivia were still snoring in the morning when Blossom made her way down to the dining room for breakfast. She brought a breakfast tray back up with a bowl of cereal, some slices of buttered toast, a glass of milk, some water, three dog biscuits and two bananas.

'Good morning, campers,' she called as she went into her room. 'I've brought you some breakfast.'

Olivia came out of Blossom's bathroom brushing her teeth.

'That was so much fun,' she said. 'I think we might do it again tonight.'

CHAPTER 3

An Argument

(Good things come to those who wait)

One summer afternoon Olivia went to call for Boris. He was sitting in the lounge watching a cricket match on the television. Olivia had packed a picnic and wanted to go to the park. Boris wanted to watch the cricket. Olivia danced in front of the TV and turned off the switch, but the tea lady put the TV back on again.

'Go and play, Olivia dear. Boris is watching the cricket match.'

'But I want Boris to come for a picnic. I've made some sandwiches for us. Cricket is boring.'

Olivia was upset. She banged the lounge door shut and went upstairs to find Blossom.

Blossom was lying on her bed with the newspaper over her face. Olivia could tell she wasn't reading the paper because it was so close to her eyes, but then Blossom started snoring gently.

Olivia tiptoed up to Blossom's bed and whispered in her ear.

'Blossom, are you awake?'

'I am now, dear,' said Blossom, lifting up a corner of the newspaper.

'I want to go for a picnic to the park, but Boris won't come.'

'Have you asked him nicely?'

'Yes, very nicely, but he wants to watch the silly cricket and won't turn the television off. Too much television is bad for his eyes and he needs to get out into the fresh air.'

'Oh dear,' sighed Blossom. 'Boris does like watching cricket. Let me look in the paper and see how much longer the cricket match is on television for.'

She turned the paper over and looked at the TV programme page.

'Another hour, Olivia. The cricket doesn't finish until after tea.'

Olivia put her head in her hands.

'An hour! My picnic sandwiches won't last that long.'

'How lovely, Olivia,' said Blossom. 'What sort of sandwiches have you made?'

'Ice cream sandwiches and they need to be eaten quickly.'

'Ah,' said Blossom. 'I see the problem. First of all, we'll put the sandwiches in the fridge before they melt, then we'll think about what to do. Let's go and sit by the fish pond and try to work it out.'

Ten minutes later Blossom was sitting comfortably in the swing chair, while Olivia walked on the wall around the fish pond.

Boris came out into the garden.

'Rain has stopped play,' he said to Blossom.

'Who is Rain?' asked Olivia.

'Rain is the solution to your problem, Olivia,' said Blossom. 'Let's have the picnic here by the pond, and then if rain starts play, Boris can go back inside.'

Olivia didn't really understand who Rain was, but at least Boris was coming to her picnic.

She ran into the kitchen and the cook gave her some picnic plates and cups, and some flowery serviettes. Olivia collected her sandwiches from the fridge and carried them out into the garden. They were all squashed together and very cold. She was examining them carefully when Boris said, 'Oh, my favourite, ice cream cake.'

Olivia looked at Blossom doubtfully, but Blossom winked and said, 'My favourite too, Boris, my favourite too.'

Blossom sliced up the ice cream cake and gave them all a piece. Olivia ran back inside to ask the cook for some chocolate sauce. Then Boris and Blossom sat on the swing chair and Olivia sat on the fish pond wall, and they ate their cake while they waited to see if Rain would start play.

'What delicious ice cream cake,' said Boris. 'I have never tasted better.'

CHAPTER 4

The Rescue

(Birds of a feather, flock together)

Olivia was sitting in Boris's room waiting for him to get ready to go into town. She liked Boris's room because it was full of interesting things: cups and medals that Boris had won for playing cricket; a clock with his name on; photographs of Boris when he was a little boy; and lots and lots of books. Some of the books were about trains, most of them were about plants and gardening, but then Olivia spotted an interesting one about birds.

'Why have you got this book, Boris?' Olivia asked.

Boris sat down on a chair to put on his shoes.

'Sometimes I go into the countryside to bird watch, and that book helps me to identify the birds I see. Look out of the window and describe a bird, then I'll see if I can tell you what it is called. You can use my binoculars if you like; they are hanging on the back of the door.'

Olivia liked using Boris's binoculars. They were special glasses that helped you to see things that were a long way away. They were old, so you had to be very careful with them and not put your sticky fingers on the glass lenses.

Olivia saw a bird sitting on the fence. It was medium size with black feathers and a yellow beak.

'What is this bird called?' she asked Boris, and described it to him.

'Ah, black shiny feathers, of medium size with a yellow beak. That an easy one, it's a blackbird.'

Olivia laughed. 'I know it's a black bird, Boris, but what is it called?'

'That's what it's called, Olivia, a blackbird.'

'Well that's boring,' said Olivia. 'Why couldn't it be called a Yellowy Beak?'

Boris brushed his hair carefully.

'Ah, this will be a tricky one for you,' said Olivia confidently. 'What do you call a little bird with a bright yellow beak, pale blue feathers, a dark blue tail and little scratchy feet?'

'A made-up bird?' smiled Boris.

'No, silly,' laughed Olivia. 'It's called a Joey.'

Boris put his glasses on and came to the window. Sure enough there was Joey sitting on a bench in the garden surrounded by a group of big blackbirds.

'They are talking to each other,' said Olivia. 'Joey is making friends.'

'I don't think so,' said Boris. 'Quick, Olivia, we have to rescue Joey. The other birds will be jealous of his pretty feathers and try to peck him.'

Olivia jumped up and ran quickly out of Boris's room, down the stairs and out into the garden. Then she stopped running and walked slowly towards the bench. The blackbirds flew away, but Joey stayed sitting on the bench looking at Olivia with his head on one side.

Olivia made the little clicking noise with her tongue like Blossom did when she was talking to Joey.

Joey stayed very still. He might even have looked pleased to see Olivia; it was hard to tell.

Olivia sat down on the bench next to Joey, and he jumped across onto her head. She didn't like that usually because of Joey's scratchy feet, but she knew she mustn't make a fuss. She stood up carefully and walked back to the door of the Home with Joey on her head.

She went into the conservatory very, very slowly and closed the door gently behind her.

'Is it cold outside, dear?' asked Hilda, looking up from her armchair.

'No,' said Olivia. 'It is quite hot.'

'Then why are you wearing your hat?' asked Hilda.

'This isn't my hat,' said Olivia. 'It is Joey. You need your glasses, Hilda.'

Hilda laughed. 'Oh dear, silly me.'

Boris puffed into the room.

'Oh well done, Olivia, you've saved Joey. How lucky that you spotted him. We better take him back to Blossom; she'll be worried.'

They went up in the lift to Blossom's room with Joey still sitting on Olivia's head, and tapped on her door.

They could hear Blossom singing.

'It sounds as if she's in the bath,' said Boris. 'We'll wait for her in my room, and then Joey will be safe.'

'Why did Joey fly outside?' asked Olivia.

'Perhaps Blossom opened the window and he wanted to stretch his legs, or should I say, stretch his wings,' said Boris, and laughed at his own joke.

'Those blackbirds were mean,' said Olivia. 'Joey only wanted to be friends.'

'Sometimes birds are like that,' said Boris. 'They are frightened of birds they don't recognise and try to hurt them, but not to worry, Joey is quite safe now, all thanks to you, Olivia.'

CHAPTER 5

Snakes and Ladders

(What the eye doesn't see,

the heart doesn't grieve over)

Olivia was sitting in the lounge of the Honey Pot Home. It was raining hard and the old people were watching a cowboy film on the television. Olivia was bored. She started to play a jolly tune on the piano, but some of the old people shushed her, so she went upstairs with Blossom to play a board game with Boris.

'What's a board game?' asked Olivia.

'A board game is perfect for when you are bored,' said Blossom.

The game was called Snakes and Ladders. There weren't any real snakes or ladders, just pictures on a big square of cardboard. You had to throw your dice, but not too hard, and then move your coloured button along the numbers. Olivia wasn't doing very well because whenever she threw her dice, the numbers seemed always to be ones or twos, but Boris and Blossom were throwing fives and sixes. Sometimes they landed on a snake and had to slide down the board a little bit, but they were both ahead of Olivia.

Then Olivia had a good idea and took her dice downstairs and into the office. She borrowed a Tipp-Ex pen from the lady behind the desk and carefully changed all of the spots on the dice into sixes. Then she went back to Blossom's room.

'Your turn,' said Boris. 'We waited for you to come back.'

Olivia threw her special dice carefully along the table.

'Goodness me,' said Blossom. 'That is an unusual dice.'

'Oh look, Olivia,' said Boris. 'You got a six. That was good luck.'

Olivia began to move her coloured button up the board. Her button passed Blossom's button, then Boris's button, and then it reached the finish line.

'Hurray. I win. I win,' Olivia laughed.

'Well done,' said Boris. 'You are good at this game.'

But then Blossom and Boris kept on playing.

'We've finished that game,' said Olivia.

'We need to see who comes second,' said Blossom.

Olivia began to fidget. Boris's button kept sliding down the snakes and going back to the beginning. Blossom nearly won, but then she went down a long snake and had to go back to the start.

Olivia did headstands against Blossom's settee.

'This is good fun,' said Boris.

Olivia went into Blossom's bathroom and began to juggle with the soaps.

'You know,' said Boris to Blossom, 'I never win at board games. Olivia must be really clever to win so easily.'

'Mmm,' said Blossom, listening to Olivia juggling the soaps. 'Be careful in there please, Olivia.'

'Whoops,' said Olivia. It went quiet in the bathroom, and Olivia came back into the room.

'I was just saying to Blossom,' said Boris, 'I wish I was as good as you at board games.'

Olivia felt a bit mean because she knew it was her special dice that had helped her to win.

She took her dice off the shelf and passed it to Boris.

'Borrow my special dice, Boris, and see if it brings you good luck.'

Boris shook the lucky dice three times and then rolled it across the table.

'Well, would you believe it?' said Blossom. 'Look, Boris, you've thrown a six.'

'Goodness me,' said Boris and began to move his button along the numbers. He overtook Blossom. He began to win. Blossom winked at Olivia.

Boris got very excited. He went along the last row of the board and then he got to the finish line.

'Goodness me. I came second. Let's have a cup of tea to celebrate. I'm going to go and get the chocolate biscuits I got for my birthday. You can have two biscuits, Olivia, because you gave me your good luck.'

Olivia swallowed, and started to explain, but Blossom put her finger to her lips to tell her not to say anything.

'What the eye doesn't see, the heart doesn't grieve over,' she whispered.

Later that afternoon, Olivia explained to Blossom about the Tipp-Ex. Blossom laughed, and said that Olivia was a clever little monkey and that it didn't really matter because Boris was happy, but to try to remember that it's better to be kind to your friends, than to always want to win.

CHAPTER 6

The Lost Purse

(One good turn deserves another)

One morning after Pip and Violet had gone to school, Olivia and Mummy walked into town to the shops. Olivia put some of her babies in the pram, covered them with a warm blanket, and took them out to get a breath of fresh air. Oo-Oo-Ah-Ah Monkey, Lottie Otter and Theo Teddy in the front of the pram, and Suzy Hippo and Reuben Giraffe in the back. Mummy was carrying Mr Wolf because Reuben Giraffe's legs were so long that they squashed Mr Wolf's paws sometimes and made him get all hot and cross.

A new shop had opened in the High Street. It was a toy shop. Olivia and her Mummy went inside to see if there was something small that Olivia could buy with her pocket money, but she was disappointed.

'I would like to get some clothes for my babies, but they don't make anything to fit,' Olivia said.

'I'm sorry,' said the shop assistant, 'but it would be hard to make clothes to fit your babies; they're all different sizes.'

'That wasn't very kind,' said Olivia to Mummy, when they went out of the shop. 'My babies can't help being different sizes.'

'Never mind,' said Mummy. 'Maybe we'll see something else for you in another shop.'

Mummy did some bits and pieces of shopping; they went to the library to change their library books, had a cup of tea in the café on the corner, and then went home.

As they walked back along their road, Olivia saw something shiny among the leaves at the side of the pavement. She poked at it with her shoe. It was a purse. Olivia picked it up and showed it to Mrs Monkey. The purse didn't have a name in it, but it did have five brand-new ten-pound notes inside.

'Oh dear,' said Mummy. 'That is a lot of money. I'll ring the police station when we get home, and let them know we have found someone's purse. We'll take it there after lunch.'

While Mummy cooked some lunch, Olivia drew a picture of where she had found the purse to help the police to solve the mystery.

As soon as they had eaten their lunch, they walked to the police station to hand in the purse. Olivia gave the policeman her map, and he said it could prove very useful. Then Mummy gave him her name and address, and described the part of the road where they had found the purse.

'The helpful map.' By Olivia Monkey.

Later that afternoon, an old lady went to the police station to report her lost purse. When she described the purse, the policeman realised it was the one that Olivia had found, and he went to collect it from the station's safe. The picture Olivia had drawn was attached to the purse with an elastic band. The policeman explained that the little monkey who had found the purse had drawn the picture. The old lady peered at the picture Olivia had drawn.

'I know that little monkey,' she said. 'She lives in the next road to me. How lovely, I'll be able to thank her myself.'

The next morning there was a knock on the front door and when Mummy opened it, on the doorstep was the old lady carrying a bright red shoe box.

'This is for your little girl,' the lady said, giving Mrs Monkey the shoe box, 'to say thank you for finding my purse.'

Mummy invited the old lady, whose name was Florrie, in for a cup of tea, and while Florrie and Mummy had a chat, Olivia opened her present.

She couldn't believe her eyes. The box was full of hand-knitted clothes for her babies all wrapped carefully in tissue paper. A stripy scarf for Oo-Oo-Ah-Ah Monkey, a pale blue skirt for Suzy Hippo, with elastic round the waist so it would be a comfy fit; two blankets: a red one for Mr Wolf and a blue one with stars for Theo Teddy; a stripy cape with lacy ribbons for Lottie Otter, and some little boots with spotty laces for Reuben the Giraffe.

'Thank you very much,' said Olivia. 'They are just what I wanted.'

'You're most welcome, Olivia,' said Florrie. 'I was going into town to buy some wool when I dropped my purse. I love knitting, but I haven't really got anyone to knit for now that my children and grandchildren are all grown up.'

Olivia dressed her babies in their new clothes, put them in the pram, and then went with Florrie round to the Honey Pot Home to show Blossom.

'What a wonderful idea,' said Blossom. 'Elsie does lots of knitting, she'd love to make sweet little things like that.'

They went to find Elsie to show her the babies' clothes.

The next time Olivia went to the home, all of the old people were sitting in the sun lounge busily knitting. They were making dolly clothes and baby clothes. Florrie was there too. She was sitting with Elsie explaining how to knit a particularly complicated pattern.

'It sounds a funny thing to say, Olivia,' Florrie said, 'but I'm pleased I lost my purse. I lost my purse but, thanks to you, I've found lots of new friends.'

'We'll be able to sell these clothes at our fete in the summer,' said Elsie, 'and all thanks to you and your sharp eyes, Olivia.'

CHAPTER 7

Lost at the Park

(All's well that ends well)

One bright summer day, Mummy and Olivia went to the park for a walk. Olivia put a fluffy old sheet into her pram and then lifted Biscuit into it. They walked down the road to the park, and Biscuit began to snore.

'There is something the matter with that dog,' said Mummy. 'He is so idle.'

'Don't be mean,' said Olivia. 'He tires easily,' and she tucked the sheet under Biscuit's chin to keep him warm.

When they got to the park, Mummy sat down on a bench to read her book, and Olivia pushed Biscuit across the grass to watch two squirrels playing in the branches of a tree. Every time Olivia got close to them, the squirrels jumped into the next tree. It was like a game, whenever she was near, the squirrels ran across the branches into the next tree, and Olivia couldn't catch them up.

Soon she got tired and sat down on the grass amongst the daisies.

'Mummy, how do you make a daisy chain?' she asked.

But Mummy didn't reply. When Olivia looked round, she couldn't see Mummy or the bench. She stood up.

'Mummy.' She stood on tiptoe. 'Mummy where are you?'

She went to the pram and lifted up one of Biscuit's ears.

'Biscuit, I think we're lost,' she whispered.

Biscuit opened one eye and looked at Olivia. Then he opened his other eye and sat up. Olivia looked upset. He scrambled out of the pram and sat on the grass next to Oliva looking closely at her face. A little tear was trickling down her cheek. He licked it away. Olivia put her arm around his neck.

'We'll stay here, Biscuit,' Olivia said, 'and wait for Mummy to find us. I can't remember which way we walked, and we might go the wrong way.'

Another mummy with two boys on scooters came along the path. The boys looked exactly the same, so Olivia knew they were twins.

'Are you alright, sweetheart?' the lady asked when she saw Olivia and Biscuit so close together at the side of the path.

Olivia didn't say anything, so the mummy asked again.

'Are you alright, sweetheart?'

'Mummy,' said one of the boys, 'the little girl doesn't know us, so she won't speak to us. Stranger danger.'

'Ah yes, how sensible,' the lady said. 'Maybe she is lost. We'll wait and see if we can see someone looking for a little girl and her dog.'

They all stood on the path looking around, and then one of the boys pointed back along the path towards the trees.

'Is that your mummy in the stripy yellow dress?' he asked Olivia.

Olivia looked to where he was pointing. She could see Mummy running down the path towards them waving.

'Yoo-hoo! Olivia. Mummy's coming. Yoo-hoo!'

Mummy ran up to them and hugged Olivia tightly.

'Oh dear,' she said. 'I am sorry. I thought you could see me. Goodness me, what a fright you must have had.'

'Thank you so much,' she said to the lady with the two boys. 'I was sitting over there, just behind that tree. I didn't realise she couldn't see me.'

'All's well that ends well,' smiled the twins' mummy. 'I need eyes in the back of my head with these two.'

She said goodbye and then walked on down the path, with the boys scooting along behind her. Olivia couldn't see the eyes in the back of her head because she was wearing a floppy sun hat.

'I'm sorry, Mummy,' said Olivia. 'I was following the squirrels and they kept jumping from one tree to another.'

'It wasn't your fault, sweetheart,' said Mummy. 'I should have called you back. We'll learn our lesson and always stay close in future. You were very sensible just to stand still and wait by the path.'

'Oh, I was quite safe,' said Olivia. 'Biscuit was guarding me.'

She put her arms around Biscuit the guard dog. Biscuit sat up very straight, and gave a squeak that was a little bit like a growl, but not a lot.

CHAPTER 8

Blossom's holiday

(Laughter is the best medicine)

Blossom was going on holiday to the countryside visit her sister, Maude. Olivia was sitting in Blossom's room helping her to decide what to pack into her suitcase.

'Where does your sister live, Blossom?' asked Olivia.

'Maude lives with her son and his wife in the Lakes, dear,' said Blossom, scrabbling in the back of her wardrobe for her best shoes.

'I thought she lived on a farm?' said Olivia.

'Yes, she does.'

'Is it a fish farm?' asked Olivia.

'Oh no, dear,' said Blossom. 'They have lots of sheep, a few cows and some hens.'

'I see,' said Olivia. 'Like Noah's Ark.'

'No dear,' said Blossom, turning round and looking at Olivia. 'Not at all like Noah's Ark.'

'It must be,' said Olivia, 'if they live on a lake.'

'Ah. I see what you mean,' said Blossom. 'The Lake District is a part of the countryside with lots of mountains and lakes, so people sometimes call it "The Lakes".'

'Well, that's a bit silly isn't it, because everyone will get confused.'

'Yes dear,' said Blossom. 'Now where did I put those Easter eggs?'

'Why do you need Easter eggs?' asked Olivia.

'For Maude's grandchildren,' said Blossom. 'I always take them a little present.'

'I didn't know you were going to see any children,' said Olivia.

'Yes, Maude's son has three children: Holly, Amy and Toby. They all live together on the farm.'

'Oh,' said Olivia. She thought for a while, and then stood up and went to the door.

'I'm going to find Boris,' she called back over her shoulder.

She found Boris in the garden weeding a flower bed that was overflowing with brightly coloured pansies.

'Blossom's going on holiday tomorrow,' Olivia said to Boris. 'She's going on holiday with some children.'

'Is she?' said Boris. 'I thought she was staying with her sister.'

'Yes, she is, and some children too: Holly, Amy and Toby.'

'Oh, Maude's grandchildren. They're more teenagers really. They'll be at school most of the time that Blossom is there.'

'So who will Blossom play with? She'll be lonely. I don't think she should go.'

'She'll be fine,' said Boris. 'She'll be with Maude. You know what Blossom and Maude like to do. They'll both chat nineteen to the dozen; they'll sit in the garden reading the papers; go for drives in the country; have tea and cakes in tea shops; and maybe send us some postcards.'

Olivia watched Boris pulling out the weeds and tidying up the pansies.

Olivia liked pansies: their faces always looked cheerful as if they were laughing.

'Pansies are always happy, aren't they Boris?' she said.

Boris smiled. 'Yes, they're very happy little flowers.'

Olivia sat on the wall next to Boris and looked around the garden.

'Boris, you know that space in the corner of the garden by the fence?' she said suddenly. 'The bit that is always in the shade, and you are never sure what plants would like to live there?'

'Mmm,' said Boris. 'That bit of the garden is rather difficult to grow things in.'

'I've had a really good idea.'

Boris sat down next to Olivia to look at the shady bit of the garden, and to hear her really good idea.

'I think we should put a sandpit there for all the grandchildren who come to visit the old people. It is in the shade, so the children wouldn't get sunburnt. If they spill the sand on the path, it wouldn't matter because it is a long way away from the lawn and the flower beds, and the children would be happy to have somewhere to play.'

'What a lovely idea,' said Boris. 'I would never have thought of that. Let's go inside and find the garden centre catalogue. We'll see if they have a sand pit that would be the right size.'

'And I'll borrow Blossom's big catalogue with toys in and put rings around the best buckets and spades,' said Olivia, and she ran back up the stairs to Blossom's room.

A few days later Mummy helped Olivia write a postcard to send to Blossom in the Lakes. On the front of the postcard was a picture of lots of smiley purple pansies. Olivia wrote:

Dear Blossom,

I hope you are having fun with Maude.

Me and Biscuit went to the park.

Love,

Olivia. xxxx

PS. I'm looking forward to you coming home.

CHAPTER 9

The Day Trip

(Too many cooks spoil the broth)

Blossom had come to Olivia's house to collect a parcel Mummy had collected for her from the Post Office. Blossom was telling Mummy about a coach trip she was trying to organise for everyone at the Honeypot Home. The old people wanted to go on a day trip, but they couldn't decide where to go. Some wanted to go to a park to have a stroll and look at the flowers; others wanted to visit an interesting historical building; some wanted to go to the seaside; and others wanted to go to see a show. It was going to be difficult to organise a trip that everyone would enjoy.

'Why don't you go to Africa?' said Olivia.

Blossom looked up in surprise.

'Have you ever been to Africa, Olivia?' she asked.

'No,' said Olivia, 'but it looks like fun. You ride in a Jeep and look at all the wild animals. It's like a zoo, Blossom, only a bit bigger.'

'Africa is a country that's far, far away,' said Mummy. 'It would take a long time to get there even if you went on a plane. You definitely wouldn't get there and back in a day. I think a coach trip to the countryside would be nice.'

'Boris gets sick in coaches when they drive round twisty country lanes,' said Olivia.

'Oh dear,' laughed Mummy. 'I can see the problem, Blossom. You'll have to do some market research.'

'What's market research?' asked Olivia.

'Well, research is when you try to find out exactly what everyone wants to do, and how much they want to do it. Then you see what is possible. If some of the old people would really like to go to a park, but would quite enjoy a trip to the seaside too, then visiting a park at the seaside might be a compromise. The research bit is finding out how much everyone wants to do what.'

Olivia went into the garden to think about the market research while Mummy and Blossom sat in the kitchen and chatted.

'Don't worry anymore, Blossom,' Olivia said suddenly, coming back through the kitchen door. 'I'll do your market research for you.'

'How kind, Olivia,' said Blossom, 'but please don't go to too much trouble.'

Olivia started her market research by tearing some pieces of paper out of her drawing pad and drawing a different picture on each sheet.

First she drew some trees and flowers to make a picture of a park, then a policeman walking for the picture of a walk, a stripy deckchair for the beach, some squares with different numbers inside for bingo, a ballet dancer for watching a show, a boat picture for a sea trip, a cake for having dinner, and a castle for an old-fashioned house.

'This is how it works,' she told Blossom and Mummy. 'Everyone has three wishes. I'll write down a number three on the back of the picture that is their best wish, a two on the back of the picture for something they would quite like to do and a one for their third wish.'

'Well done, Olivia,' said Mummy. 'You have worked hard. I really think your idea will work.'

Olivia put the pictures in her shopping bag and, when Blossom went back next door for her tea, Olivia went with her. When the old people had finished their cups of tea, Olivia stood on a chair and coughed so that everyone would stop talking and listen to her. She explained her market research, and everyone agreed that it was a very good idea.

'How exciting,' said Mabel. 'I'm going to vote for the helter-skelter. I love helter-skelters.'

'What helter-skelter?' said Olivia, looking at her pictures. 'There isn't a helter-skelter, Mabel.'

'Ah,' said Mabel. 'I haven't got my glasses on, Olivia. What picture is this one?'

'That's a policeman walking,' said Olivia. 'That picture is for people who want to go for a walk.'

'Oh, I see. I'm sorry, I couldn't quite see him properly. I hope I don't get arrested.'

Olivia looked at Mabel with a frown. 'Why will you get arrested?'

'Is this the boat trip one, dear? asked Flo quickly, picking up the picture of the castle.

Olivia put her hands on her hips. 'No, that's not the boat, Flo, it's a castle.'

'Oh yes, I can see that now,' said Flo. 'There's the flag.'

'That isn't the flag,' frowned Olivia. 'That's a soldier.'

'Oh yes,' said Flo. 'He looks very handsome. I don't want to go to a castle, so I'll give you that one back.'

Olivia sighed loudly: she could see that this was going to take a while.

Eventually Olivia had ticked everyone off her list. She took her pictures back home for Mummy to help her with the counting.

'The trees and flowers picture is going to the park. The policeman walking is when the old people want to have a stroll, a stripy deckchair is sitting on the beach, playing bingo is the numbers picture, the ballet dancer is to watch a show, the boat is for a boat trip, the cake is a nice lunch, and the castle is a trip around an old building.'

'You did give everyone lots of choice,' said Mummy.

'Yes,' said Olivia. 'Boris wanted to go bird watching, watch cricket and play golf, but he couldn't do that because I hadn't got those pictures.'

'I wouldn't worry,' said Mummy. 'Boris isn't fussy, and you can't please all the people all the time. I think you've done very well, Olivia.'

Mummy added up all the ones, twos and threes. Every picture had exactly twelve points.

Olivia was disappointed.

'That idea didn't work at all,' she said.

'Well it did in a way,' said Mummy, showing Olivia a brochure that the postman had delivered that morning. 'This brochure is for a seaside resort. A coach could get there easily on the motorway so Boris wouldn't feel travel sick, but just look at the pictures.'

Olivia sat down and looked inside the brochure. The seaside place had a lovely shady park with beautiful overflowing flower borders, and brightly coloured deckchairs clustered around a bandstand. On the bandstand, a lady was singing in front of a brass band. Lots of people were sitting in the deckchairs watching her and eating ice creams. At the end of the park, there was a crazy golf pitch, and a wide promenade with lots of seats, different types of cafés and bingo arcades; and then a long strip of sandy beach. A little way out to sea was an island with a castle in the middle and a ferry boat setting off from a pier to cross over to the island.

Olivia laughed. 'That is perfect, everyone will be happy with that, even Boris. He can take his binoculars and look at all the sea birds; he can sit on a bench and watch the people playing cricket on the beach, and then me and Boris can go and play crazy golf. Oh, and look at the end of the pier, there is even a little fun fair with a helter-skelter for Mabel.'

'Everyone's a winner,' said Mummy, laughing.

CHAPTER 10

Going to the Cinema

(Every cloud has a silver lining)

It was twelve days after Christmas and Olivia was feeling upset. Daddy had gone back to work, Pip and Violet had gone back to school, and Mummy had started to take down the Christmas decorations. Olivia had asked Mummy if they could be left up until her birthday, but Mummy said that it was bad luck to leave the decorations up for too long and anyway, the decorations would begin to look tatty after a while.

Olivia went to the Honeypot Home so that she wouldn't have to watch Mummy and be sad, but when she went into the home, the old people were taking down their decorations too. Their lovely Christmas tree was leaning against the door that led into the garden ready to be shredded, and Olivia felt as if she was going to cry.

Blossom was sitting in the lounge with Mabel.

'Oh dear, Olivia, what's wrong? You have a face like a wet weekend,' smiled Mabel.

'Would you like to come to the cinema with us?' Blossom asked. 'Mabel and I thought we might take a little trip into town. We've just looked in the paper and there is a good film on at the Odeon.'

'What's the Odeon?' asked Olivia.

'It's the name of the cinema in town,' said Blossom.

'What's the cinema?' asked Olivia.

'It's a bit hard to explain really,' said Mabel. 'Rather like a big television in a huge hall.'

'That sounds like fun. I'll go and ask Mummy if I can come,' said Olivia. 'Don't move until I come back.'

'We wouldn't dare,' laughed Mabel. 'I do hope your mummy says yes.'

Mummy said that it was a lovely idea, rang Blossom to check the arrangements and gave Olivia some money for her cinema ticket. On her way out of the house, Olivia picked up Mr Wolf because he was looking a bit sad too.

'Come on Mr Wolf,' she said. 'Cheer up. It's not the end of the world.'

'I'm back,' said Olivia, skipping into the lounge.

Mabel and Blossom were being silly and sitting very still, and then when Olivia came back, they started to talk again.

'Just pulling your leg,' smiled Mabel. 'You did tell us not to move.'

'You can't possibly reach my leg from over there, Mabel,' Olivia laughed. 'What a silly thing to say.'

Mabel and Blossom put on their coats and scarves, and they all went out of the big front door and into the street.

'This will be good for us,' said Blossom. 'It's nice to be out in the fresh air.'

They walked quickly to the cinema because it was rather chilly.

Mabel paid the man at the desk in the cinema foyer, and they went through some big doors into a huge dark room. There were rows and rows of red seats facing a big screen.

Blossom chose a row of seats.

'You go in first, Mabel,' she said, 'and then Olivia can sit between us.' Mabel chose some seats in the middle of the row. Olivia took off her coat, then she took off Mr Wolf's hat, put him on the arm of her chair and sat down between Blossom and Mabel.

When Mabel took off her coat, she accidentally knocked Mr Wolf off the arm of the chair.

'Ooops, sorry, Mr Wolf,' Mabel said. 'It is a bit squashed in here.'

Then she took off her scarf, and accidentally hit a man's head sitting in front of them He turned round and tutted-tutted.

Olivia got off her seat to find Mr Wolf.

'What's the matter, Olivia?' said Blossom.

'I'm saving Mr Wolf,' said Olivia. 'Mabel knocked him onto the floor.'

Mabel began to giggle, and Blossom frowned at her.

'Come back up, Olivia, sit on your seat, dear, the film is about to start.'

Olivia looked around.

'My seat has gone, Blossom,' she whispered.

'What's the matter now?' said Blossom.

'My seat,' said Olivia. 'It's gone, it was here a moment ago and now it's gone.'

'It's a tip-up seat,' said Mabel. 'When you're not sitting on it, the seat tips up.'

Blossom held Olivia's seat down for her. Olivia climbed back up and sat Mr Wolf carefully on the arm of her chair, and then the film began.

It was an exciting film about a clever princess and a silly wizard. The wizard kept trying to put a spell on the princess and change her into a frog, but the princess was always too clever to be caught out. Olivia really enjoyed it.

When the film ended, Mabel, Blossom and Olivia walked back home. Olivia hadn't been out at this time of night before and everywhere looked very different. The roads were dark; shiny street lights were on, and Olivia could see into the rooms of the houses as they walked past.

When they got back to the Honeypot Home, all of the Christmas things had been tidied away and everywhere looked clean and bright. Fresh flowers were in big vases on all of the tables, and new plants were in the pots standing in the hall. Daddy was sitting in the lounge with Boris waiting for Olivia.

'New year, new start,' smiled Blossom.

'Thank you for coming to the cinema with us, Olivia,' said Mabel. 'It was such good fun. Maybe we could all go again sometime soon.'

'Yes please,' said Olivia, 'I don't feel sad anymore. I really enjoyed myself at the cinema.'

CHAPTER 11

The Fete

(Every man has his price)

It was the day of the Honeypot Home's Summer Fete. Olivia was very excited. She and Daddy got up early to go and help set up the stalls. Daddy was moving tables out into the garden at the back of the Honeypot Home, and Olivia was helping Boris to lay out all of the plants he had grown on the plant stall.

There were going to be lots of interesting things for the visitors to do: a bouncy castle, pony rides and a coconut shy. Elsie was setting up a stall with dolly and baby clothes. Helen was running a book stall; Fred was in charge of tombola; and Mabel was in charge of a 'Guess how many sweets are in the jar' competition. There were ice creams and cream teas, raffles and some old-fashioned games like:

'Knock the tins of the shelf', 'Lucky Dip' and 'Bounce a ping pong ball into a goldfish bowl'.

After a while Olivia began to get bored with helping Boris; he was being a bit fussy about putting all the same plants in the same row, so she went to have a look around the rest of the stalls. Elsie spotted Olivia and waved to her.

'I'm so pleased to see you, Olivia,' she said. 'I wonder if we could borrow some of your babies as models for dollies' clothes please. Everything looks a bit boring just lying on the table. If your babies could model the clothes, people would be able to see them more easily.'

Olivia hurried home and put her babies in the pram. Mr Wolf, Lottie Otter and Theo Teddy in the front of the pram, and Suzy Hippo, Reuben the Giraffe and Oo-Oo-Ah-Ah Monkey at the back. Then she went back to Elsie, lifted the babies onto the table for Elsie to dress, and parked her pram neatly under the table.

Olivia and her babies.

O O-oo-Ah - Ahs
scarf

olivia

reuben giraffe
and shoes.

Theo teddy
and his
blanket

'You better go and help Boris again, Olivia,' Elsie said. 'He looks as if he's getting a bit flustered.'

Daddy came to help Boris as well and soon the three of them had the plant stall organised. Boris had to answer questions about the plants that the visitors wanted to buy: what their names were and how to grow them. Olivia's job was to wrap the plants carefully in pieces of old newspaper, while Daddy took the money and lifted anything heavy.

Then the gates were opened and in came all the visitors. It was soon very busy and Boris's plants were selling quickly.

'We're making lots of money,' Daddy said. 'How lucky the Honeypot is to have you, Boris, and your green fingers.'

After a while, most of Boris's plants were sold. Daddy gave Olivia some money to spend at the other stalls. She bought a pretty scarf for Blossom from the Nearly New stall; a book about trains for Boris from the Book Stall; a box of dominoes for her to play with Daddy; a yo-yo for Pip and a bouncy ball for Violet from the Toy Stall, because they looked as if they would be fun; and some clip-on dangly earrings for Mummy from a lady on the White Elephant stall.

'Oh dear,' said the lady on the White Elephant stall, 'you are getting a bit over loaded. Let me find a bag for you, sweetheart.' And she put all of Olivia's things into a big brown carrier bag.

On her way back to Boris and Daddy, Olivia passed Elsie's stall.

'Thank you so much for letting us use the babies as models,' Elsie said. 'Would you believe we've sold all of the dollies' clothes. I'm sure it was because everyone could see how well they fitted different animals.'

Olivia took her pram out from under the table and pick up her babies to put in the pram. Lottie Otter and Theo Teddy in the front of the pram and Suzy Hippo, Reuben the Giraffe and Oo-Oo-Ah-Ah Monkey at the back. Something was wrong. The pram didn't look right. Someone was missing.

'Where's Mr Wolf?' Olivia asked Elsie.

'Oh, he must have fallen down somewhere,' said Elsie, and they looked under the table and round on the grass, but they couldn't see him.

'Your Daddy must have him,' said Elsie. 'He did look after my stall for a while when I went to get some more change from the office.'

Olivia hurried back with the babies to Daddy. He was lying in a deckchair next to Boris's stall having a little snooze.

'Wake up, Daddy. Mr Wolf is lost. This is an emergency,' said Olivia.

'What? Who's lost?' said Daddy, sitting up quickly and looking around.

'Mr Wolf is missing. Have you got him?'

'Your friend Ruby's little brother Jamie, bought him from Elsie's stall.'

Olivia began to cry.

'Oh Daddy, Mr Wolf is my baby. He wasn't for sale.'

'Don't cry, Olivia, I'll find him and bring him back. Don't worry, it will be alright. You stay here with Boris. I saw Jamie's mummy with Ruby and Jamie by the bouncy castle: I bet they are still bouncing.'

Daddy hurried away.

Olivia sat down next to Boris.

Boris smiled kindly at her.

'Don't worry, Olivia, we know exactly where Mr Wolf is. It won't take us long to get him back.'

Sure enough, two minutes later Daddy re-appeared with Jamie. Jamie was pushing his tricycle and, there sitting in the basket, was Mr Wolf.

Olivia could feel Mr Wolf watching her anxiously.

'There's been a mistake,' Olivia said to Jamie. 'Mr Wolf wasn't for sale, and I need him back now please, Jamie.'

Jamie looked at Mr Wolf. 'He's fast asleep and I can't wake him up.'

Olivia sighed, and looked at Daddy. Daddy looked as if he didn't know what to do.

'I have a good idea,' said Boris, and he winked at Olivia so that she knew that he had a plan that would make everything better.

'We can do a swap, Jamie,' said Boris. 'What have you got in your great big, exciting present bag, Olivia, that you can swap with Jamie for Mr Wolf?'

Olivia thought about the things she had bought. They were all nice things, but she needed to rescue Mr Wolf. She knew he would feel travel sick in a tricycle basket. She could always buy other presents, but she could never get another Mr Wolf.

She laid out all her presents on the grass.

'I will swap any of these great big, exciting presents for Mr Wolf,' she said.

Jamie looked at Olivia's things carefully, and then pointed to the clip on, dangly earrings.

'Excellent choice,' said Daddy. 'I couldn't have chosen better myself, young man.'

Jamie gave Mr Wolf to Olivia, and Daddy clipped the earrings onto Jamie's ears, and he pedalled off across the lawn on his tricycle.

Boris, Daddy, Olivia and Mr Wolf watched Jamie heading back towards his mummy. Then they all looked at each other and began to laugh.

'Come on, Olivia. We'll go to the stall and get some more earrings,' said Daddy. 'You were very good not to make a fuss. All's well that ends well.'

They went to the White Elephant stall and when the lady heard the story about Mr Wolf, she gave Olivia two sets of earrings for Mummy, wrapped in coloured tissue and inside pretty little boxes.

'This is because I think you are very kind,' she said. 'Your mummy will be proud of you, but I think she will laugh when she hears about Jamie and his earrings.'

CHAPTER 12

The Fancy Dress Party
(Great minds think alike)

Olivia had been invited to her friend Rebecca's birthday party. It was going to be a fancy-dress party.

Olivia went to the Honeypot Home to show Blossom the invitation. Blossom was sitting in the sun lounge with Hettie and Boris listening to some music on the radio.

Olivia explained all about the party.

'How lovely,' said Hettie. 'Who are you going to be?'

'What do you mean?' said Olivia.

'Well, if the party is fancy dress, you have to choose someone to dress up as.'

'I don't think so, Hettie,' said Olivia. 'Fancy dress means you wear a party dress.'

'It does sound as if that is what you would do,' explained Blossom, 'but fancy dress means dressing up as someone or something else. Maybe a doctor or an astronaut or a farmer. Or perhaps someone from a nursery rhyme like Little Miss Muffet or Old King Cole.'

'Oh, I see,' said Olivia thoughtfully, 'but I don't know who to be. This is going to be difficult.'

'Not really,' said Hettie. 'You can have so much fun deciding on your costume. Is there a character in a book that you particularly like?'

'That's a good idea,' said Blossom. 'Perhaps Paddington Bear or Peter Pan.'

'When I was a little boy, I went to a fancy-dress party as a cowboy,' said Boris, 'with my mother's felt hat and my father's checked shirt.'

'Do you have anything useful in your dressing up box, Olivia?' asked Blossom. 'I've got lots of shawls and jewellery you could borrow. Maybe you could be a Spanish lady or a fortune teller?'

'Oh, yes,' said Hettie, 'and I've got a collection of hats that might be fun. We could make you an Easter bonnet, and you could be the Easter Bunny.'

'Then I borrowed my mother's washing line to make a lasso,' said Boris.

'You've got lots of good ideas,' frowned Olivia, 'but I just need one really good idea.'

'Maybe you could dress Biscuit up as something, and use him as a prop,' said Hettie.

'Sleeping Beauty perhaps,' laughed Blossom.

Olivia looked at Blossom.

'Or perhaps he could be your sheepdog and you could be a shepherd,' Blossom said quickly. 'You could borrow a floppy hat from Hettie's hat collection and put some straw in the brim.'

'But if Biscuit was Sleeping Beauty, who could I be?' asked Olivia.

'You could be Biscuit's prince,' said Hettie. 'I've got a little red jacket with gold buttons that would look very smart. We could make you a sword from cardboard and silver paper.'

'Then I took my sister's toy sheep, painted some black spots on its back, and pretended it was a cow,' laughed Boris.

'Perhaps you could borrow something from Pip or Violet that would help,' said Hettie.

'How about being an imaginary character?' said Blossom. 'A robot or a fairy?'

'I made myself a sheriff badge with card and silver paper,' said Boris.

'I expect lots of Rebecca's friends will go as fairies,' said Hettie. 'It would be good to go as something a little bit unusual. Maybe a television set or a teapot. How about a chocolate muffin cake?'

'Oh yes, good idea,' said Hettie. 'I've got a red beret that could be the cherry on your head.'

'And I wore my father's waistcoat over the shirt,' smiled Boris.

'Olivia dear, Daddy's at the door. It's your tea time,' Fred called from the hall.

'Did Blossom give you some good ideas for your fancy dress?' asked Daddy as they walked home.

'Yes and no,' said Olivia. 'She and Hettie had so many ideas, they made me a bit confused.'

'How about being a footballer?' said Daddy. 'That would be easy. You can borrow one of Pip's old football kits. You won't have to worry about keeping clean or spilling ice cream down your front. You can just run about and have fun.'

'That's a good idea, Daddy,' laughed Olivia. 'I'll be a footballer.'

Pip said that Olivia could borrow one of his old football kits.

'It might still be a bit big for you, but you can tuck the top into the shorts and roll the socks down. It will be fine.'

Pip had two old kits, one was a red shirt with white shorts and the other was a blue and red shirt with blue shorts. Olivia decided that the red and white kit suited her best.

Olivia had a lovely time at her very first fancy-dress party. She got ice cream down the front of the football shirt, and cake on the shorts, but Daddy put the kit in the washing machine after the party and it came out good as new.

The next morning an invitation popped through the letter box inviting Olivia to her second fancy-dress party.

Daddy laughed out loud when he read the invitation to Olivia. The invitation was from Blossom and Hettie to a fancy-dress party they were organising at the Honeypot Home.

Postscript for teachers

For a free resource pack to accompany three of the stories from 'Olivia and the Proverbs', please contact: -

https://patguyschoolandfamily.com/

The resource pack provides worksheets and activities to support the development of: -

- Attention and concentration
- Visualisation
- General knowledge
- Vocabulary
- Empathy
- Reading comprehension

The pack is appropriate for use with literacy and nurture groups, in addition to providing support materials for PHSE and study skills lessons.

ABOUT THE AUTHOR

The author is a mother of four and a grandmother of seven.

Pat Guy called upon her experience of child rearing and teaching young children when writing this book. The author's teaching experience, expertise and interest lie in the field of literacy acquisition and development.

Printed in Great Britain
by Amazon

22449602R00062